I0788104

NOLA AND THE MAGIC TURTLE

Mikala Hari

Mike Jones

It's a beautiful day. The sun is shining brightly, and birds are chirping in the tree. And... someone is waking up! She's moving left, right, and then she wiggles her toes.

Who is waking up? Oh, look, it's Nola! Her big brown eyes are blinking. It's a new day, Nola, let's wake up and play!

Now, after putting on a purple dress and your favorite socks, it's time to go.

Meghan and Shai are here, too! They are Nola's Mom and Dad. They love to run around with Nola. And they love to throw a little red ball to her, back and forth. Back and forth.

Oh, look, some little animals want to play, too. Who are they? There is Mr. Bird. He likes to sing. Can you sing also?
And there is Mr. Worm, who likes wiggle. Do you want to wiggle, too?

And there is Mr. Turtle. Oh, hello, Mr. Turtle, what do you do?
Mr. Turtle is slow, but he is also magical. Mr. Turtle's name is Omar.

Listen carefully, Omar Turtle is talking. Shh, he is whispering. What are you saying, Omar Turtle? What are you saying?

Oh, he wants us to come to a special place. Hold on tight, he says. But, Mr. Turtle, you are soooooooo very sloooooow.

Nola, Mom, and Dad hold on tight to Mr. Turtle. And suddenly, in a bright golden flash, they are gone!

Where do they go? Oh, there they are! They are flying over the sea with so many big blue waves. They fly over the Bahamas and over Cuba, too.

But wait, now they are on Omar Turtle's back. Floating in the water, going up and down. Up and down. Can you see

What are you saying, Omar Turtle? What are you saying?

He is saying, "Look, there it is! Look, there is Jamaica!"
Nola, Mom, and Dad stand up and wave.
They wave their hands up so high. Up so very high!

Why? Because all the people on the beach are waving.
"Wah gwaan?" they say. "Wah gwaan?"
That means, "How are you?"

And Nola, Mom, and Dad are so happy. So, they smile
and say, "Irie!" IRIE! WE ARE GOOD!

Omar, the magic turtle, floats to the sandy shore with Nola,
Mom, and Dad on his big strong back.
Everyone is dancing and clapping. It is a celebration.
A party to welcome Nola and her family.

Can you dance? Wiggle back and forth? Can you clap?
Hands together... clap, clap, clap!

Omar Turtle says, "These are my boonoonoonoos friends!"
This means Nola, Mom, and Dad are very special to him.
Can you say boonoonoonoos?

More wiggles more claps, and now it's time to eat.
We have some fried fish and festival! There's carrot juice
and sorrel. What about jerk chicken and fried dumplings?
Maybe some plantain?

It is so yummy to our tummy. Let's lick our lips, eat our food,
and laugh with Omar Turtle and friends.

And then it is time to say goodbye. So, hold on tight,
Nola, Mom, and Dad. Omar Turtle is ready to go!

We say goodbye to our Jamaican friends and family.
Likkle more! Mi gone mi gone!

Mi gone mi gone!

And now we go. Hop on our turtle's back, over the sea,
we float, and back home to our backyard.

Oh, what a day, Nola! We wiggled, giggled, and danced.
We ate, laughed, and danced some more.

Now let's say goodbye to Mr. Turtle, our little friend Omar,
who has so much magic in his tiny turtle shell.

Bye-bye! Likkle more!

SHCHERBATOVA SVETLANA

FEDERICA DE FALCO

END